LAB COAT GIRL
in MY TRIPLE-DECKER HERO

LAB COAT GIRL
in MY TRIPLE-DECKER HERO

Margie Palatini

Is anybody in there?

L. A. F. :)
Books

Hyperion Books for Children
New York

First Edition
1 3 5 7 9 10 8 6 4 2
This book is set in 13-point Cantoria.

Library of Congress Cataloging-in-Publication Data
Palatini, Margie.
Lab Coat Girl in my triple-decker hero / Margie Palatini.—1st ed.
    p.   cm.—(L.A.F. books)
Summary: Experimenting with different combinations of foods,
Trudie continues to try to make her fellow fifth grader Ben fly
and develop other superhero powers.
ISBN 0-7868-2442-5 (hardcover)—ISBN 0-7868-1348-2 (pbk.)
[1. Flight—Fiction. 2. Size—Fiction. 3. Science-Experiments—
Fiction. 4. Schools—Fiction.] I. Title. II. Series.
PZ7.P1755 Lh 2000
[Fic]—dc21 00-038480

CONTENTS

Super Supreme

Chapter 1

THE FORMULA

* *From the secret Lab Coat Girl notebook:*

*What yours truly, Trudie Marks knows
absolutely, positively — up to this
moment in time :*

*Subject A, Benjamin Bonekowski (AKA Benjamin Bone)
and Subject B, yours truly – 'moi' (that's 'me'),
Trudie Marks (AKA Gertrude), (AKA Lab Coat Girl),
have produced and exhibited
(— boy! have we produced and exhibited)
unusual (understatement)
chemical reactions .*

(cont. on next page)

The aforementioned reactions
manifest themselves when subjects
are in the company of one another.
(Either accidentally — or by mutual choice.)

* This reaction happens when :
    Subject A (Ben) <u>eats</u>

Result : Subject A (Ben)
        becomes what he eats
        (LITERALLY)

Conclusion: Ben + Trudie = Amazing!

note: experiments can produce
        unexpected results

formula: Ben + Trudie + Carbonation =

Up! Up! and Away!

TODAY IS THE DAY ↑

Chapter 2

COUNTDOWN

Ten.
  Nine.
  Eight.
  Seven.
  Six.

"Hold it! Houston, we have a problem!"

Houston, we have a problem? Again? The boy just didn't give up. I looked at Ben with his white-knuckled, two-handed grip on the lawn furniture.

"*Now* what?" I walked over from "control central" (aka the picnic table) and sighed, "This is the fourth time in two minutes that you've delayed liftoff. Would you pul-ease get with the program, Bonekowski? We're losing light here."

"Cool your jets, Gertrude," said Ben, still holding the wrought iron as if his life depended on it (which, okay, maybe it did). "I'm a nanosecond away from floating off into the wild blue yonder with only this string you call a rope to yank me down to earth. I want to make sure I make the return flight without cracking my cranium."

How was I ever going to make a superhero out of Benjamin Bonekowski when he was so stubbornly earthbound? Where was his sense of adventure? Risk? Reckless abandon?

I wondered if Orville ever had this much trouble with Wilbur? Or was it Wilbur who had trouble with Orville?

memo to yours truly . . .
Find out what's right with Wright.

"Trudie? Earth to Trudie: Are you listening to me? I want another safety check."

Another safety check. I was beginning to

sense the "fizz" portion of my equation was working against us in the "fearless" department. I had fully expected the "float" part of my formula calculation to kick in by now and just sweep Ben up in the "magic of the moment." (Let's face it, flying without the benefit of a plane is definitely magical.)

I checked the rope and knots around Ben's waist. Again. For the seventeenth time that afternoon.

We had no time to waste. The window of opportunity to get Ben airborne was only as long as my father's nap on the living room couch and my mother's trip to the grocery store.

Considering that my brother, Stuart, was tagging along with Mom, and how easily the little guy was prone to cart tantrums—plus the very real mathematical probability that our cat would and could jump on my father's stomach at any moment—this experiment had very little room for error at this end.

An untimely Stuart wa-wa, followed by an even more untimely diaper disaster or fat-cat pounce, meant the very real possibility that Ben and I might be found out. Not to mention, grounded for life. Parents are pretty earthbound, too.

"Everything's A-okay," I told him. "I've checked and triple-checked the checklist. And look what I'm doing," I said, reaching into my pocket. "A safety pin. There." I pinned it to his shirt. "Now you're completely safe."

"You're a real comedian, Gertrude," he said, tightening the rope himself, "I just want to make sure that I walk out of here on the two legs I walked in on. The big soccer game against Mountainview is in two weeks, or have you forgotten?"

"Who can forget when you've been reminding me every five minutes. Get focused. This is science, not soccer."

Ben repinned the pin. "Look me straight in the eyes, Trudie. Are you sure—no—really, really, really positive you're going to be able to reel me back in? There's no chance that I'm going to be lost in space, right?"

I took off my glasses and stared Ben straight in the pupils. I put both hands on his shoulders. I smiled—showing teeth.

(Make a note: Showing teeth is totally sincere.)

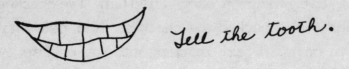 *Tell the tooth.*

I flashed a wide, toothy grin. "I promise. There is no danger of your being lost in space. You're not even going to leave the atmosphere. The rope is only sixty feet long. Your space is limited to the backyard. Now just take it easy and relax."

Ben was sweating. Upper-lip sweating. He was not relaxed.

"What, I ask you, what are you worried about? You drank the formula, right?"

Ben burped. "Check."

"You haven't diluted yet, right?"

Ben patted his backpacked water bottle. "Check."

"You're feeling light-headed and light-footed, right?"

Yes, we could both see his tippy-toes were already very tippy.

"Check."

"And you're very anchored."

Ben tugged on the rope. An elephant, never mind Ben, couldn't budge that wrought iron.

"Check."

"Okay," I said clapping my hands. "Now, just let the 7UP do the work, will you? What could go wrong? This lawn furniture weighs a ton and this is a new rope. What's the mathematical probability of that unraveling?"

Ben winced. "Did you say *unraveling?*"

"No unraveling. Forget I said that. Concentrate on up, not down. Don't worry. Look. See right over there?"

Ben turned as I pointed. "The pile of leaves I raked is all set for your landing. Safe and soft."

"That looks more crunchy than soft, Trudie. Couldn't we throw on a few pillows over there? How about some of these cushions from the furniture?"

"Cushions. Who needs cushions? You're going to land feet first."

"I am? But . . . But—suppose my feet don't come down first, or—"

"Ben, Ben, Ben! Trust me. This is a no-brainer."

"But . . ."

"Ben. A 7UP float. Rope. Leaves. I've got this levitation formula down to a 'duh.' Stop worrying. You, Benjamin Bonekowski are going to be the first human being in the entire course of history to fly. I mean really fly. For the love of Albert Einstein—we are fifth graders defying gravity using carbonation and milk products!"

I straightened my glasses and loosened his grip on the wrought iron. Color slowly returned to his knuckles. I gave him a pat on the back.

"Now, get up there, make history, and enjoy the view—while that formula is still fresh."

I didn't want to take any chances that those carbonated bubbles would go flat. A flat formula might equal a flat Ben. A Ben going *blat* right in the backyard would be most difficult to explain to Coach Perkins and the soccer team. Not to mention our parents.

I returned to my position at control central. "Ready?" I called out.

Ben nodded and shut his eyes.

Five.

Four.

Three.

Two.

One.

Chapter 3
FLY BOY

Ben let go of the top of the lawn chair one finger at a time. And then slowly . . . slowly . . . inch by inch. Foot by foot. Up. Up. Up. Yes! Yes! Ladies and gentlemen, we had liftoff! We had liftoff!

"We did it! We did it!" I shouted as Ben floated higher.

Ben opened his eyes. "Hey! Look at me!"

He waved down to me as he swayed in the breeze. He floated over the garage roof, then drifted above Stuart's jungle-gym swing set.

"We did it, Ben!" I began scribbling notes and scrambled for my pocket camera. "We did it!"

"To infinity—and beyond!"

"Don't go too beyond," I warned him. "Just stay in the backyard. And don't get too close to that big maple in the corner. We don't want you to get tangled up in the branches."

I snapped a few shots from the left. The right. Then the left again. Then centered underneath him. Someday, these little pocket shots were going to be in history books. Now, we needed to proceed to firsthand observations and make accurate recordings.

"What's it like up there, Ben? How do you feel?"

"It's great. And I feel terrific. *Very light!*"

Lighter than air. Of course. I knew that extra squirt of "light cream" was going to do the trick. Did I know my secret formulas, or what?

Trudie Marks :

Super Supreme Secret Formula Maker.
    (*seriously*)

"Squawk! Peep! Peep. Peep. Peep."

Great. My astronut was talking to the birds.

"Ben, stop fooling around, and start taking notes. You have to chronicle your observations.

We have to note any significant changes in bodily functions."

"Trudie, I'm up in the air. I think that's a change in my bodily function. Wow! This bird thing is all right. I bet I can see a couple of miles from up here. I bet I can see ol' Mountainview from here. Watch out, you Mountainview Hawks—" Ben stretched his arms out in front of him. "The Amazing Benjamin Bone is here to swoop down and beat your butts!"

"Stop showing off. This is a scientific experiment. You're supposed to be making critical observations."

"Yeah, yeah, yeah. Okay. Take note. The sky is still blue, the grass is still green, and I can see Mr. Seligman mowing his lawn."

"Mr. Seligman?" I said, almost choking as I gulped. "From all the way down the street? He didn't see you, did he? Duck! This is a top-secret experiment."

"Duck? How am I supposed to duck when I'm floating forty feet off the ground?"

"Nosedive!" I shouted.

duck?

"Nosedive? Wait a minute. Don't you crash when you nosedive? I don't want to nosedive!"

"Then, dip! Somersault! Do something. We can't let anybody see you flying!"

I grabbed the rope and gave a hard yank. Ben bobbed up and down. Down and up. Ten times in a row. I think I might have just overdone it a bit in the yanking department.

"Whoa! Stop!" Ben shouted. "I'm getting airsick! Look out below! Do you want me to barf up my fuel and crash?"

I immediately gave the rope more slack.

Ben put out his arms and steadied himself in the breeze. "DO NOT, I repeat, DO NOT pull on that rope like that again. One more yank and you're going to be wearing ice cream soda spew."

He made his point. Gross. But very visual. Fortunately, Mr. Seligman finished mowing and all threats to our top-secret flyboy experiment were gone. I gave him more rope.

"There you go," I called up to him. "You're flying and fabulous!"

"Well, yeah, I'm up in the air, but I wouldn't exactly call this flying."

I put my hands on my hips. "What are you talking about? You're in the air. That's called flying."

"It's hovering, not flying."

Hovering. All of a sudden Benjamin Bonekowski was an expert in aerodynamics. Yours truly, Trudie Marks, has the power to lift the boy off *terra firma* with nothing but an ice cream soda, and he's quibbling about definitions.

"I'm more like a balloon than Superman," he whined. "Shouldn't I be moving around—fast—instead of just floating?"

"So move. Start flapping."

"Superman doesn't flap," Ben argued. "Birds flap. Superman zooms. He puts out his arms, jumps, and zooms. Faster than a speeding bullet, remember? Able to leap tall buildings in a single bound. I'm not speeding or bounding anywhere." Ben held out his arms. "Look. This is not zooming. How can I be a superhero if I don't zoom? All I am is a human version of the Goodyear Blimp."

Yeesh.

The boy just did not understand the complexities of science.

Blimp. Honestly. What an exaggeration.

Well, okay . . . So, maybe he was more blimp than superhero. I supposed the formula could use a minor tweak or two. The zoom factor did look like it needed an adjustment or two. The Amazing Benjamin Bone couldn't very well save anybody from imminent disaster at the speed of a slug. And we were definitely going to have to ditch that rope. I'm pretty sure there's never been a super-hero with a rope tied around his waist. David Letterman was sure to pick up on that.

Okay. A little tweaking was on the "to do" list. Still, I think anybody would have to agree that getting Benjamin Bonekowski airborne with nothing more than a 7UP float was an unbeliev-able and amazing success. And someday, when we were ready of course, the entire world would know it, too.

"Trudie!" Ben suddenly shouted in a panic. "Stop! Abort! Get me down from here!"

"What? Why? What's wrong?"

"Reel me in! *Now!* Clear the way for immedi-ate dilution and elimination!"

"What happened? Did a bird peck you?" I shouted up to Ben. "Did Mr. Seligman see you? . . . Oh, no. Is my mother coming?"

"Worse," yelled Ben. "The worst. Zoey Appleton and Sarah McCarthy are walking up the street and they're heading this way."

I dropped my notebook. "SCRUB THE MIS-SION!"

Chapter 4

OH BOY, HOUSTON, DO WE HAVE A PROBLEM!

Zoey and Sarah were my two best friends since forever. Truly.

They also could not keep a secret. Double truly.

About anything.

And Ben flying like a bird definitely came under the heading of "anything." Ben had to get back on solid ground. Now.

"DIP! DIVE! DO SOMETHING!"

"Reel me in! Quick!" Ben shouted as I grabbed hold of the rope and yanked as hard as I could. "WHOA!" he cried out, as I covered my head against possible upchuck.

Ben made like a bird. Then a fish. He flapped, swam, kicked. He was stalled in midair! I pulled and tugged. But for every yank down, the rope slipped a bit and went up.

"They're almost at the driveway!" Ben cried as he kept kicking and flapping while I pulled and tugged.

Down. Down. Down. He was getting closer to me. Closer. Closer.

"Get my hand!" Ben shouted.

I reached up but couldn't touch his fingers. Then he did a backward somersault. Luckily, halfway through his backflip I grabbed his left pant leg. I yanked as hard as I could.

"Oowwwww!" Ben cried out as we both landed with a thud nowhere near the planned leaf-pile touchdown site. Then, before we knew it, he bounced up again.

"Help!" he shouted on the rebound.

I gave another yank on the rope and jumped to grab his pant leg. I reached up, put my arms around his waist, and wrestled him to the ground.

Then I completely immobilized him in the only

way I knew how . . . I sat on him.

"Gertrude, get off of me! And get this rope off, too!"

Ben pushed me off and began untying the knots.

"WAIT! No! Ben, WAIT! You have to hold on to something!" I shouted as he became ropeless. "You haven't diluted yet! You're still at full-strength carbonation! Ben, you're not anchored!"

Liftoff number two.

"Oops," Ben cried as he bounced, bobbed, and began floating.

"Anchor!" I shouted. "Anchor!"

Unfortunately, the way Benjamin Bonehead decided to anchor himself was not by holding on to the chaise lounge. Not by holding on to the chairs. Not even by making a desperate grab for the cement planter full of dying geraniums. What he decided to hold on to for dear life was—yours truly.

And—just as Sarah and Zoey walked into the backyard.

"What are you two doing?" asked Sarah,

looking at us with a weird expression on her face.

Ben's face was as red as one of those geraniums. "Uh, uh . . . Wha-wha-what are we doing, Trudie?" Ben stammered.

"What are we do-do-doing?" I stammered back trying to come up with some logical explanation for which there was no logic. Sarah and Zoey were staring at me. "Practicing soccer," I finally blurted out.

"Soccer?" said Zoey.

"That's right. Ben was, uh, tackling me. I mean, I was tackling Ben."

Zoey smiled. "You don't tackle in soccer, Trudie."

"That's right, Trudie," said Sarah.

"THAT'S RIGHT, TRUDIE!" repeated Ben, as he gave me a poke.

"Well, maybe it wasn't exactly soccer."

Ben and I slowly twisted out of the bear hug and walked arm in arm over to a chair on the patio. (Well, I walked. Ben floated tippy-toe style.) I pushed him down into the seat. He got a ten-fingered grip on the bottom of the chair with both hands.

"What is *really* going on with you two?" asked Zoey. "You've been acting weird ever since Vander's birthday party."

"Even before that," said Zoey. "You two have been acting weird ever since you were partners for Mrs. Hicklemeyer's project."

"Hey, that's right," said Sarah. "What are you two up to, anyway?"

"*Up* to?" Ben grinned. "Did you say, *up* to?" He looked at me and started to laugh.

"*Up* to?" I repeated unable to stifle myself.

"What's so funny?" asked Zoey. "Are you keeping some kind of secret or something?"

We tried, but we couldn't stop laughing. And then, right in the middle of a belly laugh, Ben suddenly burped. It was a whopper. His grip ungripped and it was pretty evident that the "float" in the formula was about to kick in with another carbonated liftoff.

There was only way to keep Ben from being airborne in front of Zoey and Sarah. There was only one way to keep this top-secret experiment top-secret. I had no other choice. This was science.

I sat down on Ben's lap.

Zoey's mouth was open even wider than before. I looked at Sarah. Her mouth was open too. I looked at Ben. His mouth was very open.

"I'm tired. I had to sit down," I said, offering an explanation.

"But on *him*?" said Zoey.

"On him?" said Sarah.

"ON ME?" cried Ben, as his face got red and his ears became blotchy.

Just as Ben was about to push me off his lap, we both felt a rumble from beneath our seats. We knew that one more burp from Ben, and Sarah and Zoey were going to witness the first lawn-chair launching in history.

We both knew I wasn't going anywhere.

The two of them began to giggle. "O-o-oh, o-kay," Sarah said. "I get it. Zoey, I think we'd better leave now. It looks like these two want to be *alone*."

Alone? Did she just say *alone*?

"NO! We don't want to be alone!" I said. "Are

you kidding? Ben and me. Me and Ben. Alone?"

Ben and I looked at one another. We both still felt very "floaty."

"Well, uh . . . maybe . . . we do," I mumbled.

"Then, so long, you two," Sarah singsonged. "We are out of here."

"Definitely," said Zoey.

They turned. They walked. They were going . . . *And* they were giggling. There was nothing Ben and I could do but stay silent and chair-bound as they walked out of the yard. Still giggling. Girl giggling.

I knew full well what that kind of giggling meant. I was a girl. I had done plenty of that sort of snickering myself.

This was not good. Not good at all. This was disastrous. By tomorrow everyone at Martin Van Buren Elementary was going to think that Ben and I . . . ugh. I couldn't even say it. Everyone was going to think that we actually liked each other.

"Bye-bye, you two," called out Zoey as she and Sarah disappeared around the corner of the house.

"Water. Water! Get me water!" Ben shouted, pushing me off his lap and jumping up from the chair.

He made a flying leap over to the picnic table and hung on to the umbrella pole with both hands. His legs floated up and became horizontal, and then he began waving like a flag.

"Help!" he whimpered, as his pant legs flapped in the breeze.

I scrambled up off the ground, grabbed the water bottle, and stuck the tube into his mouth. Ben sucked down the H_2O until the formula was diluted enough for him to stabilize and stand on his own two feet. He stared at me with those squinty eyes that he thinks scare me.

This time, he was right.

"Now look what's happened, you loony Lab Coat Girl!" Ben shouted after another big gulp from the water bottle. "Sarah and Zoey think that you and I—that we—us—oh, yeeck! This is the worst mess your weird science has gotten me into yet!"

For once, I agreed with Ben. Total P'tooey!

This was the end of Lab Coat Girl and the

Amazing Benjamin Bone. Forever.

Trash "Plan B," and say so long to David Letterman.

Ben + Trudie = Amazing

Chapter 5

HE SHOULD HAVE HAD A V8

I bunched up two pillows and punched another. Very hard. I flopped down on my bed and stared at the ceiling in my room.

This was awful. Terrible. Ugly. Not just plain ugly; very ugly. Our Ben-plus-Trudie equation was way out of control.

I didn't care if we were amazing. I didn't care if we were making history. *David Letterman Show* or no *David Letterman Show*. Science or no science. There were just so many sacrifices a girl scientist was expected to make. And having everyone think that I liked Benjamin Bonekowski, was not, I repeat, NOT one of them.

Yeeck.

What was I going to do? I told myself, think, Trudie, think. Think. Think. THINK.

I couldn't think. My brain cells must have been in shock.

There was nothing left but to make an attempt at some damage control. I got off the bed, walked down the upstairs hall, and speed-dialed Zoey. I figured I would just tell her that Ben and I were . . . what? How was I going to explain all of this?

Ben and I were being funny? . . . Uh-uh.

Ben and I were being cool? . . . Don't think so.

Ben and I were being . . . dumb?

Dumb, looked like the number-one convincing explanation for her finding us hugging. What else was there? My only alternative was to tell her about our amazing chemistry and our top-secret experiments. But that was top-secret.

The phone started ringing. Two. Three. Zoey picked up.

"Hi, Zoe," I said, hearing her voice on the other end of the line. "It's me, Trudie. . . . About this afternoon. I bet you've been thinking all sorts of . . . uh, Zoey? . . . Zoe? . . . Zo-e-e-e-y. Are you there? Zoey? Zoey?"

She didn't answer. She was laughing so hard, she couldn't catch her breath.

I hung up.

Uglier than ugly. This was superugly.

That settled it. Ben and I were through. Finished. No more experiments. Ever. Forget that yours truly, Trudie Marks, may have just changed the entire evolutionary process. Forget that I got Benjamin Bonekowski airborne on a couple of sips of carbonated soda and a scoop of ice cream. Forget that, for the lack of a little zip, zap, and zoom, I was a squinch away from creating a totally real superhero for the new millennium.

Ben and me. Me and Ben. Over. So over. I was going to stay away from Ben, and Ben was going to stay away from me. That was that. Our chemistry was history.

I went back to my room and plopped down on my bed. I rolled over and looked at Albert. He stared back from atop a pile of wood chips in the corner of his cage.

"Albert, I've made my decision. I'm going to concentrate all my scientific efforts on growing some hair for that tail of yours."

I put my nose close to the bars and went eyeball to eyeball with the little rodent. "Bald may be beautiful where Michael Jordan is concerned, Albie, but you are going to be the first rat with more than just fuzz on your tail. And that's a promise."

Fuzz-Tailed
Albert ←

Albert looked extremely happy at the news. He

scrambled into his wheel and started those four tiny legs and four itsy pink feet going a mile a minute. He was like a little engine full of energy.

Now, that's what you call a rat with zip, zap, and zoom, I thought to myself.

That's when it hit me.

It was so simple. So completely obvious. How could I have missed it? No wonder my flight formula produced more balloon than bird. It was all float and no zoom. The flyboy formula needed a power boost. Some juice. An "engine." Of course. Ben should have had a V8!

I jumped off the bed and hurried to my desk. I booted up the computer and opened my "Plan B" secret superhero file.

Trudie + Ben + carrots/spinach + carbonation (preferably) 7-up + ice cream (float) =

★ ⭐ Super Ben ⭐
★

I scrolled. Typed. Calculated.

Yes. Yes. Perfect. All the ingredients were there now. Power. Boost. Lift. Zoom.

That was it! The superhero formula! All in one superduper gulp. Superstrength. Supersight. Superflight.

The exact amounts, of course, most likely still needed a bit of adjustment here and there. But yes, I was certain, this was it. Spinach plus carrots plus a veggie-zipped-up secret flight formula equaled—superhero! Add a little "fast food" to the equation, and nothing was going to stop the Amazing Benjamin Bone.

"Trudie Marks, you've done it!" I yelled.

And then . . . I remembered. To do it, I needed something else. I needed Ben.

Oh, glory Galileo.

This science-fame-and-fortune thing was getting very complicated. How was I going to continue the experiments with Ben without Zoey, Sarah, and everybody else thinking that he and I . . . I mean me and him . . . I mean . . . us . . . we . . . Oh, boy. This was complicated, all right.

I looked over my shoulder to Albert and sighed.

"Albie, what am I going to do? I can't be amazing unless I make Ben amazing. And I can't make Ben amazing unless we spend time together. And if we spend time together, everybody in school is going to think . . . well, you know. Albert, my secret scientific career could prove socially embarrassing. What should I do?"

Albert stopped spinning the wheel and looked at me with his wonderful little all-knowing rat eyes. I walked over to the cage, reached in, and picked him up. I sat him down on my palm. I rubbed behind his ears, which always made him especially happy. Albert's nose twitched and his whiskers almost curled.

We looked at each other and pondered the problem.

Albert always gave the best advice. He was one rat with all of his feet on the ground.

"You're absolutely correct, Albert," I said as he wiggled his nose and his pink tongue licked my fingers. "What am I thinking? How can I even question it? This is science. You can't have success unless you have failure! Albert, you're right. A lab coat girl's gotta do what a lab coat girl's gotta do."

Albert and I looked at our reflections in the mirror.

"They can all laugh if they want, but I'm not giving up."

Albert wiggled his nose in agreement.

Now I just had to convince Ben.

Chapter 6
KICKS

I decided the best tactic was to lie low and avoid Ben for at least three full days. (Note: Three is always a good number.)

This was not a difficult course of action, as Ben must have decided on a similar plan himself. Then again, we had done this routine a few times before in the last few weeks. Ben already had plenty of practice at ignoring me from the time I turned him into a baby. A hot dog. A suck-up. A cat. The Incredible Bulk. Well, okay, you get the picture. So there were some glitches. It was to be expected. We were dealing in weird, uncharted science, after all.

We sat at opposite ends of the bus. We made absolutely no eye contact in Mrs. Hicklemeyer's class. I stayed a safe distance behind him in the cafeteria line.

By the third day of not paying the least bit of attention to each other, even Zoey and Sarah had stopped giggling. The "like" factor became a nonissue. (Which was a relief.)

Ben and me. Me and Ben. It was not that funny. Seriously. Truly. It wasn't. Yucky, most definitely. But not funny.

memo to yours Truly . . .

B + T ← *Not Funny!*

I figured that after seventy-two hours, Ben just might be approachable again. I was right. The strange thing was, I didn't have to approach him at all.

I saw from the corner of my eye that he was sitting only two seats behind me on the bus. I could see over my shoulder that he was just a few steps behind me, following me down the hall to homeroom. Then I noticed that only two lunch trays separated us in the cafeteria line. And then, two periods later . . . he spoke.

Nobody was more surprised than yours truly at that one. Our class was walking to the gym for P.E. when suddenly I heard—

"Psst. Trudie. Psst."

Of all the psst-ers in all of Martin Van Buren, I wasn't expecting Ben to be one of them. Especially psssting up to me. But he was.

"Hi. Hey," he said. "What's up?"

"Up?"

"Oh, yeah. Up."

We laughed as Ben walked alongside me, but of course, kept a respectably safe distance.

"Uh, you know, Trudie, I've been thinking," he said.

"Really? What a coincidence. I've been thinking, too." I stopped walking. "What have *you* been thinking?"

Ben stopped, too. Then we both took a few steps closer to the corridor wall. "Me? Well, uh . . ." Geoffrey Kuperman passed by. Then

Bonnie and Willa, Vander, Jamie and Grant, followed by Andrew, Alex Fortunato, and finally Timmy Schoenfeld.

"I've been thinking," Ben whispered as the last person in line, who just happened to be Zoey Appleton, was now a safe distance in front of us. She looked over her shoulder at us, then turned and hurried up to the front of the line to Sarah. We watched them run off giggling.

"Oh, no," I moaned. "Not again."

"Never mind about them," Ben said with a shrug. "I think it's dumb for us to be not talking and ignoring each other."

"You do?"

"Sure," Ben continued as we took a few slow steps toward the gym. "What do we care what they think, right? We know that we don't like each other . . . I mean, like *that*."

"Absolutely!"

"We're just friends."

"Totally."

"Hey, we're not even friends. We're more like, uh . . . uh . . . whatever you call it."

"Yes. More like that," I agreed.

"You know, Trudie, we can't let what some people might say about us get in the way of science."

I couldn't believe what I just heard come out of the mouth of Benjamin Bonekowski. He sounded almost "dedicated."

"Ben, are you saying what I think you're saying? You still want to continue with—" I whispered. "'Plan B' and our superhero experiments?"

Ben's face was a blank. "Huh? 'Plan B'?"

"You know," I said with a subtle arm flap.

The lightbulb went on. "Oh, 'Plan B'. The experiments. Yeah . . . Right."

"Great. And, don't worry. I've figured it all out now. I've calculated a new, improved formula. It's foolproof. Ooh, I should have brought my notes. But never mind—I have it practically all memorized—boost, lift, zoom. What you need to eat is—"

"Whoa. Whoa. Whoa!"

"Whoa, whoa what?"

"Slow down, that's what."

"But you said you wanted to do the experiments . . . didn't you?"

Ben opened one of the double doors to the gym and we walked inside, heading for the locker rooms. He was stammering. He was stuttering. He wasn't saying he would do it.

"I . . . I . . . I just think we should . . . ease into it, that's all."

I looked at him suspiciously. "What do you mean, ease into it?"

"I'll tell you after we change," he said running toward the boys' locker room door. "Meet you in the middle circle on the floor in five minutes."

We were in our gym uniforms, standing a safe distance from each other so that Sarah and Zoey wouldn't start up one of their giggle fits, when Mr. Perkins blew his whistle. "Okay, people. Let's choose up sides. This is practice for the big game next week."

Ben looked over to me. He smiled. "Soccer."

"Soccer?" I silently mouthed the word.

Ben walked over and stood next to me. "Just stay close."

"Listen up," said Mr. Perkins, standing in front of the group. "We only have two more practices before the game with Mountainview next week.

We know they're a good team. They're a very good team. But just remember, we are, too. We can win this championship!" His voice echoed in the gym. "So, let's be sharp. Let's be quick. Let's be the best we know how to be. Now, let's have a good practice out there!"

The coach clapped his hands and blew his whistle. Then he began counting pairs and assigning kids to their practice squad.

"Blue team: Harris. Newman. Ross. Morrisey. Kramer. Levin. Greer. Petersen. Red: Stevens. Witlow. Bonekowski. Marks . . ."

Ben gave me a nudge as Mr. Perkins continued calling out names. "Come on. Follow me. And stay close."

"Stay close? Why do you keep saying that?" I took a few steps back. "Wait a minute. What are you up to, Bone?"

Ben smiled. "Trudie, I'm a good soccer player. You're a good soccer player. But do you have any idea how great we could be together with . . . just the right—diet?"

I folded my arms in front of my chest and nodded. "So that's it. You don't really want to do something for science. You want to do it—for you."

"Me?" Ben sounded shocked. "For good ol' Martin Van Buren is more like it. Where's your school spirit, Gertrude? Our school hasn't beaten Mountainview Middle School for ten years. Think of it, Trudie. With just a little bit of extra chow gobbled down next to you, I could be the next—"

"What? You-a-ham?"

"Huh? Me? A ham?" He looked at me as if he didn't know what I was talking about, and then laughed. "Me a ham. Mia Hamm. I get it. Hey, that's good, Trudie. Put that on the menu. I hadn't even thought of that myself."

"What exactly did you think of yourself?" I asked suspiciously.

"For starters, how about a triple-decker hero sandwich? Triple-decker. Hero. I ate it for lunch. Pretty smart, right?"

"So that's why you've been getting closer to me all day. On the bus. Down the hall. In the cafeteria line. You've been using me, Bonekowski! You've been eating behind my back!"

"That is harsh, Trudie. Very harsh." Ben reached into his pocket and pulled out a handful of something.

"Hey! Now what are you eating?"

"Watch. It can't miss," he mumbled stuffing his mouth.

"Just a nanosecond," I said running alongside of him. "What are you eating?"

"Primo cereal, Lab Coat Girl."

Cereal? I didn't get it. It couldn't be corn flakes. Too corny. Too flaky. Puffed rice was a definite no-no. What was Ben eating?

"Trudie, you're not the only one who can come up with formulas you know," Ben said, sounding very smug. "I've done some calculating on my own. I figured that with a hero sandwich—no bologna of course—a 'breakfast of champions,' a morsel or two of Kix, a bit of Special K, and some Lucky Charms, I should be able to score a goal all the way from the backfield! Just so you're next to me, that is. Together we are the Martin Van Buren Bulldogs' secret weapons!"

Before I could say I wasn't sure if I wanted to be a secret weapon, Ben ran up to the ball and kicked it.

Wow. All I can tell you is . . . cereal really works.

Chapter 7
DON'T DRINK *THAT* WATER!

"Holy cow! What a kick!" yelled Oliver.

"That was incredible!" shouted Geoffrey Kuperman with a burp.

"That was unbelievable!" cried Timmy, running up to Ben.

"That was amazing!" said Mr. Perkins.

Uh-oh.

"Bonekowski," Mr. Perkins called out from the sidelines. "Let me see you do that again."

"Stay close," Ben called to me over his shoulder as he ran up to the ball that Mr. Perkins had just tossed onto the field. Ben focused. He took a few steps. Ran. Kicked.

Boy, did he kick!

The ball soared in a huge arc right across the

field and flew into the net. Oliver threw Ben another ball. Ben did it again. And then again. Six times straight. Mr. Perkins couldn't believe his eyes. Neither could anyone else.

Then we did practice drills. Ben was . . . well, you know . . . amazing. He dribbled, he stopped, he dribbled, he cut, he kicked, he headed. Then he kicked the ball across field and ran so fast—he actually passed to himself! He kicked. He scored!

Oh, yes. He was definitely *amazing* all right.

Everyone on the team jumped all over him— he was a genuine hero, all right. A triple-decker hero. And this was only practice.

"I think we might have a chance next Tuesday," said Oliver as we all headed for the locker rooms after practice.

"Might?" said Grant with a laugh.

"Yeah. We're going to win!" shouted Michael, running up to Ben and slapping him on the back.

"We're going to do it, right, Ben?" Geoffrey called out as he headed into the locker room.

Ben grinned. "You know it!" He looked at me and whispered, "Pretty amazing, huh?"

I followed him across the field. "But, Ben, you

and I know why it's amazing. It's our secret chemistry. And I'm not sure we should be using our special powers to win a soccer game."

"Why not?"

"Why not?" I said, still running beside him. "Because it's . . . it's . . . sort of . . . I don't know . . . not legal."

"Not legal?" Ben made a face. "What are you talking about? What's not legal about eating breakfast cereal?"

"I'm serious, Ben. We will be winning not on our own merits. I have to really think about whether I want to be part of this," I said pushing on the door to the girls' locker room.

"What's to think about?" Ben said as I went through the swinging door. "You want us to win the biggest game of the past decade, don't you? Well, don't you?" The door swung closed. "Trudie? . . . Trudie?" I could hear him call out from the other side of the locker room door. "Hey! Don't you want us to win?"

Ben was waiting right outside the door after I changed.

"You are going to stay close to me, right,

Trudie? I mean, during the game, that is. You're not going to let the whole team down, are you?"

"Ben, I'm not sure it's fair to win a game because of our special abilities."

"Special abilities is what sports is all about, Trude," he said, following me down the hall to class.

I turned and looked over my shoulder. "But your special abilities are . . . you know, very special. I don't think it's . . . fair."

"Fair? *Fair?* You didn't think about fairness when it came to the school elections. Or the big Hicklemeyer project. Or being on *The David Letterman Show*! How come you didn't think about being fair all of those times?"

I admitted that was true. But that was before we knew the full scope of our abilities. "No, I've made my decision. As much as I want us to beat Mountainview, I think we should direct our scientific focus to bigger things that benefit all of humanity."

Ben walked in front of me and stopped. "What are you talking about? This benefits humanity. It benefits the entire school! We win!"

I walked around him and headed back to home-room. "Winning isn't everything. You should know that already from what happened in the school elections."

"Listen to you! Lab Coat Girl suddenly has a conscience. Where was your sense of fair play when you fed me cat food and meowing became my second language?"

I shook my head. "Not going to do it."

"Trudie. Please. I was ready to eat birdseed for you, for pete's sake!"

"No. And that's that."

"Is that your final answer?"

I groaned and kept walking. But Ben was relentless. He wrote me two notes during math. Five in Spanish class. He pestered me on the bus all the way home. Called me three times. E-mailed me twice. And then finally cornered me in the cafeteria line at lunch the next day.

"Please, Trudie? Please? Please? Please? Come on. Say you'll stay by me for the good of ol' Martin Van Buren. Just think how happy you can make every student in the school. And all you have to do is—nothing."

I pushed my glasses all the way down my nose and looked at Ben. "Nothing?"

"Just stay close to me—not even that close. A little close. We won't even use our full-strength powers, how's that? I won't eat that super sub I was planning to eat. No triple-decker hero. Not even a double-decker. No decker."

"Ben . . ."

"Just you, me, and the cereal—and don't forget, I'm still going to do 'Plan B' with you. Anytime. Anywhere. You. Me. Up. Up. And away." Ben leaned close and whispered. "The bird thing, remember? Superhero stuff? And anything else, too. Anything at all for you and science. Consider me your lab rat. I mean guinea pig. Sorry. I didn't mean to offend Albert."

Since when was Ben ever worried about offending Albert? I moved along the cafeteria line and put a plate of meat loaf and mashed potatoes on my tray. I picked up a fork and knife from the silverware bin, then reached for a juice carton.

"You're being unusually cooperative and sensitive," I said, picking up a straw. I bit off the top and blew off the paper. "In fact, you're being uncommonly nice—for you."

Ben smiled. "I only want what you want."

We got to the cashier and before I could put my hand into my pocket, Ben paid for my lunch. As in—used his own money.

I grabbed his arm. "That's it. Okay, what have you been eating now, Benjamin Bonekowski?"

"What makes you think I've been eating something, my dear friend Trudie?" He picked up my tray and carried it—without my asking—over to my lunch table. "Why wouldn't I want to do something for the finest human being on the face of the earth?"

"You have been eating something, haven't you?" I said following right behind him. "What was it? Charms? Was it charms? Candy? It was some kind of candy, wasn't it? That's why you're being so sweet."

"Oh, so I ate a couple of bars of chocolate," he whispered.

"BEN!" I gritted my teeth and tried to remain

calm, cool, and collected.

"Don't panic. I was careful," he said with an unusual confidence. "I know the drill. I didn't eat any Baby Ruth's or anything with nuts. I'm not crazy, you know."

I sighed with some sense of relief. Then I looked at him and wasn't so relieved anymore. Something was different about him. Very different. And it had nothing to do with Ben acting nicer than usual either. In fact, I was pretty sure the sweetness in him was wearing off fast and something else was taking over.

Ben barely put down the tray between Zoey and Sarah before I grabbed him by the arm.

"Hey! Hey! What are you doing?" Ben asked, as I dragged him over to the trash receptacle in the corner of the cafeteria.

"What am *I* doing? What are *you* doing?" I said in a loud whisper. "Look at yourself."

He looked. "Yeah. So? What?"

"So, aren't you usually *taller* than I am?"

"Of course, I'm taller." Ben looked *up* at me. "YIKES! What's happening? I'm . . . I'm . . . I'm . . . Oh, no. I'm shrinking!"

tiny!

Oh, yes. Ben was getting smaller right before my eyes.

"Let's get out of here," I said, pushing him out of the cafeteria.

"Look at me! Look at me!" Ben cried out as he tripped on his pants, which now looked two sizes too big for him. "What did you do to me this time, Trudie Marks?"

"What did I do? You're the one who's been making up his own formulas."

"Formulas? I ate food! All I did was eat candy!"

"What did you eat?" I asked him as he dropped another three inches. "WHAT DID YOU EAT?"

"I told you. Just a couple of chocolate bars."

"Show me the wrappers! SHOW ME THE WRAPPERS!" I shouted as his chin began disappearing beneath the collar of his shirt.

Ben pushed up the sleeves of his shirt and found his right hand. Then he reached down—way down—into his pants pocket and pulled out a bunch of crumpled candy wrappers.

I grabbed them from his now chubby little

six-year-old-looking fingers and flattened out one of the wrinkled wrappers.

I gasped. "These are *miniatures*! You ate miniature candy bars!" I started counting. "One, two . . . three, four . . . five. Six. You ate seven miniature candy bars!"

"Oh, no!" cried Ben. "I'm a mini-me!"

"That's right, you shrunk yourself, you bone-head! Quick. Over to the fountain and start drinking water before you're the size of an ant!" I grabbed his hand and began dragging him down the hallway.

Then the bell rang. Lunch was over. In about five seconds the hallway would be crammed with kids. There was no way Ben's little legs were going to carry him to that water fountain in time.

So I did.

"Put me down, Trudie!" Ben squirmed as I held him and his oversized clothes in my arms.

"Quit your wiggling. I know what I'm doing. I've been carrying my little brother since he was born. I'm not going to drop you . . . I think. Hey? Where are you?"

I looked down the neck of the shirt. "Are you still there?"

From somewhere down deep inside the flannel shirt and rumpled khakis I heard a faint squeak. "Water. Water. Quick!"

This was critical. Time was of the essence. If I didn't get some water into the boy immediately, there might be no boy left to get water into.

The hallway was getting crowded with kids trying to get to class. There was no way the hall water fountain was going to work now. Not in his condition. We needed somewhere private. Someplace we could be alone. Someplace where we could be absolutely sure nobody would interrupt us.

There was only one place in the school to fit that description.

There it was.

I pushed open the swinging door and ran inside. But before Ben had a chance for even a glug or gulp, we heard footsteps. Voices. I ran to an open cubicle and locked the metal door with a clank.

I hung the shirt and pants on the hook on the door and did a quick frisking. "Are you okay in there?"

"Where am I?" came a squeaky voice from somewhere down inside the pants. I saw something wiggle. Then a little head with a very dizzy look poked out from the back pocket. Ben looked around. He shook his head and blinked.

"Am I where I think I am?" Ben asked. Then he looked down. "Oh, no, Trudie, I am not drinking *that* water!"

Chapter 8
SHRINK·WRAPPED

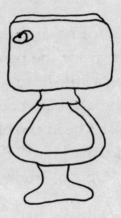

"I am not drinking toilet water!" Ben squeaked.

"Of course you're not drinking *that* water!" I whispered. "Did I ask you to drink that water?"

"So what am I doing next to a toilet bowl, Miss Lab Coat Girl?"

"This is an emergency. I had to hide you someplace, didn't I? Well, this is it!"

"But I need water!" Ben cried. "To drink! If I shrink any more I'm going to disappear!"

"I know that. Don't you think I know that? Hey. I've got an idea. I think I've got something here." I reached into my pocket and pulled out a roll of Life Savers. I quickly peeled back the paper with my teeth. I gave it to Ben. "Here. Suck on that. It should stop the shrinking process—I think—I hope—until you can drink some water, dilute, eliminate and get back to normal."

"But, I don't like peppermint."

"Just do it!"

"Okay. Okay," he said, holding the Life Saver like an oversized doughnut and taking a lick.

Ben was now the size, give or take a few millimeters, of Albert. Talk about amazing! If I had only had my tape measure with me to accurately record the exact shrinkage.

"Now, Ben, don't panic, but I think it could be just be a little tricky getting you back to normal."

"What? What about water equals dilution equals elimination?" he squealed.

"Yeah, well . . . I don't know exactly if—"

"TRUDIE! I can't stay like this," said Ben. "You've got to change me back. Now! How am I

59

going to play soccer? How am I going to do any-thing? Holy cow. What time is it? If I don't show up in class, Mrs. Hicklemeyer is going to think I'm cutting school. She'll call out an all-points bulletin on me. I'm going to get suspended! Expelled!"

"Will you please forget soccer, Mrs. Hickle-meyer, and getting expelled? You have bigger things, I mean smaller things, I mean you've got enough to worry about. You're fish bait!"

Ben looked at himself. "Yikes! I am fish bait!"

"Just keep sucking on that Life Saver. Stabilize. Stabilize—and shhh! Quiet. There are people out there. I think I can hear Willa. Bonnie. Zoey."

We heard giggling.

"Oh, great. How long is that going to take?" he moaned.

The girls room door opened. "Ladies?" said a voice. It was Mrs. Hicklemeyer. "The bell is about to ring. Everybody out."

I heard more talking. Then foot shuffling.

Then—a knock. On my stall door!

"Excuse me. Whoever's in there . . ." called Mrs. Hicklemeyer. "Class is starting in one minute."

I didn't answer.

"Excuse me. You in there? Are you okay?"

Well, that was debatable. "Okay" compared to what? The definition of okay totally depended on one's perspective of this whole situation. Scientifically, this was more amazing than anything that happened to either of us before. And that included flying.

Of course, parents- and teacher-wise this was a whole other story. I didn't know what the reaction would be to a pocket-sized fifth grader. However, I kind of figured it would be better if I never found out.

I looked at Ben sucking on his peppermint Life Saver. Luckily, it seemed to have stopped his shrinking for the moment. More good news. His breath had to be fresher than it had ever been in his life. However, fresh breath or no fresh breath, I had to figure out a way to get him back to normal, and ASAP.

"I said, are you okay in there?" Mrs. Hickle-meyer asked, knocking on the door. The clothes and Ben swung back and forth. Ben dropped the Life Saver, lost his grip on the edge of the pocket, and fell inside.

"Holy Galileo!" I cried out hoping there wasn't a hole in those pants for Ben to slide through.

"Trudie? Trudie Marks? Is that you?"

"Oh . . . Oh . . . yes, Mrs. H. It's me. Trudie."

"Are you all right?"

"Well, actually . . . no. I'm not feeling too well. I think it was . . . the meat loaf. Yup. I'm sort of sick. My stomach. My head . . . my, you know . . ."

"Oh, dear," Mrs. Hicklemeyer answered in a worried-sounding voice. "Let me get the nurse for you."

"No! No!" Ben squeaked softly shaking his head back and forth peeking out from the pocket.

"Did you say no, Trudie?" said Mrs. Hickle-meyer.

I put my pinky over Ben's mouth and muffled his squeaks. "No, I mean yes. Yes. Please get

Mrs. Terwelp. And maybe she should call my mother to come and pick me up. Oooh. Oooh. Hurry, Mrs. Hicklemeyer. Hurry!"

We heard the click of Mrs. Hicklemeyer's shoes on the tile floor and the whoosh of the swinging door.

"What do we need the nurse for?" squealed Ben. "What I need is water!"

"We don't have time to fill you with enough water to counteract all of those mini candy bars you gobbled down. You're so small, I don't know how long it's going to take to get you back to your regular size. I've got to get you to my house so we can work on the dilution and elimination equation."

"But why do we need the nurse?"

"How do you think we're going to get you out of here? I can't very well carry you and your clothes home on the school bus, can I?"

"But, how are you going to get me home without anyone seeing me like this?"

"I'll put you in my backpack."

"Trudie. I'm naked! I did all the shrinking, and my clothes stayed the same."

I ripped a few sheets of toilet paper from the dispenser and stuffed it down into the pocket with Ben.

"Here. Wrap these around you like a towel. That should work until we get back to my house."

Ben crawled down into the pocket with the sheets of crumpled tissue paper.

"Trudie, don't look!"

"Honestly! Really! Get a grip! Who wants to look?"

"Well, don't!"

"I'm not! Just keep quiet, you little pip-squeak!"

"Hey!" Ben squealed poking his head outside the pants pocket. "Who are you calling pip-squeak?"

"If the shoe doesn't fit . . ."

"Trudie? Trudie? Did you say something?" Mrs. Terwelp called out as the girls' room door opened with a whoosh. "Are you all right?"

"Flu, Mrs. Terwelp," I said from the bathroom stall. "I think it's the flu."

"Oh, my," said the nurse. "I called your mom and she will be here as soon as possible. It's never a good thing when we become ill while in school, is it? Why don't you come back to the infirmary with me? Perhaps you will be more comfortable there?"

I looked at Ben still stuffed in the pants pocket hanging on the door hook.

"Uh . . . I . . . I . . . I . . . don't think I can make it all the way down the hall, without, well . . ."

"That's fine, dear. I understand."

I sighed with relief. Luckily nurses know all about indelicate oopsies and don't require long, detailed, gross explanations.

"Trudie, if you're okay to leave alone, and you would prefer some privacy, I'll go down to the office and wait for your mother."

Ben nodded his head in agreement.

"In fact, I'm waiting for several parents," the

nurse continued. "There are at least half a dozen students in the infirmary right now with symtoms just like yours. It's getting so crowded down there, I almost can't keep track of everyone who's there."

What luck. That was just the information Ben needed to avoid being suspended.

"I think, Ben Bonekowski wasn't feeling too well, either, Mrs. Terwelp. He must be one of those kids who's going home early, too."

"Benjamin? Hmm. I'm not sure. But . . . uh . . . yes, I think he may well be one of the boys in the office, if he isn't one who hasn't been picked up by a parent already."

I looked at Ben and sighed. "You just go back down to the office, Mrs. Terwelp. I'll be fine." Then I groaned a few more times and sounded very weak. "Ooh. And could you bring me my backpack, too, Mrs. Terwelp?"

"Backpack?"

"I . . . I . . . I don't want to get behind with my schoolwork," I answered.

"Trudie, I'm amazed you can think of work when you're feeling so poorly. No problem, dear.

I'll be back with your mother as soon as she arrives. You'll be home, safe and sound, in no time."

Ben gave a mini thumbs-up. I sighed with exhaustion and sat down on the you-know-what.

Chapter 9
BEN AND KEN

I stuffed Ben's pants, shirt, two huge smelly sneakers (yuck), underwear (double yuck), as well as mini-Ben himself into my backpack without the nurse getting suspicious. I also had to moan, groan, and act like I was about to barf my brains out.

The things I do for science.

My mother finally arrived, signed me out, and then Ben, the backpack, and yours truly were outta there and heading for home.

I was semi-relieved. At least my usual poop-in-my-pants-like-I-was-two-type panic had passed. I unzipped the bag and peeked inside to check on Ben.

I saw books. I saw pants. I smelled sneakers. I didn't see Ben.

Cancel "semi-relieved," fast-forward again to panic.

"Ben? Ben?" I whispered frantically hoping to hear any sort of wayward squeak. "Are you in there? Are you all right?"

I heard a crumpling. Felt some wiggling. Saw a ripple down in the toe of Ben's left sneaker. The ripple moved from the toe, under the laces, past the tongue and finally Ben climbed out from inside of the beat-up Nike. I held my nose, held out my thumb, and gave him a hoist.

"I'm okay. I think," he whispered back, holding on to the edge of my fingernail. "All that bumping up and down in here is like being on a roller coaster. And if that smell inside my sneakers didn't kill me, nothing will."

"Don't worry. Everything is going to be okay."

Then, of all the worst possible times, Stuart decided not to take his usual forty winks while strapped into his car seat. Wide-awake, he spied mini-Ben's little head peeking out of the back-pack.

"Mouse!" he squealed.

"Mouse?" My mother looked at us from the rearview mirror. "What's your brother talking about? What's going on back there, Trudie?"

"Mouse! Mouse!" Stuart repeated, getting all excited and drooly.

"Nothing." I pushed mini-Ben back inside his sneaker. "Nothing's going on." I said quickly, zipping up the backpack, as Ben squeaked and Stuart squealed. "Stuart, Shhh. Don't be silly. There isn't any mouse."

"Mouse!" the little squirt insisted.

"No mouse!" I said, plugging his pacifier in his mouth with one hand and tossing the bag on the floor of the car with the other. Out of sight, out of his little mind. At least long enough to get home and get Ben and that backpack up to my room. And before anyone found out that I had shrunk Benjamin Bonekowski to the size of an action figure. A toilet-tissue-wearing action figure.

The car pulled into the driveway. I grabbed the backpack and scrambled out of the car. Then before my mother could manage to lift Stuart from the car seat, I lugged the backpack and myself into the house.

I pounded up the stairs, ran into my bedroom, closed the door shut, and slung the bag onto my bed. I yanked the zipper, and dumped the contents out onto the bed.

"Hey! Hey! Watch it!" Ben squeaked. He somersaulted across the quilt and got up clutching his toilet-tissue towel. "That belt buckle almost knocked me out, Dr. Frankenstein."

"Sorry. Are you okay?"

"Am I okay? Look at me. Of course I'm not okay!"

"Let me get my notes and review the formula equations."

"Forget your notes!" he wailed holding tight to his tissue. "I need water, remember, Lab Coat Girl? Water equals dilution equals elimination equals back to normal. Get me back to normal! How am I supposed to play in the big game like this?"

That was a problem all right. Right now, Ben's game was more like miniature golf. With Ben being the ball. Before I got him back to soccer-playing size, I had to at least get him back to trike-riding size. Or at the very least big enough to use training wheels.

Personally, I thought being the size of Stuart Little was absolutely fascinating. The idea of traveling around in someone's pocket all day, or scrambling around behind walls, scooting over pipes sounded fabulous. Who could ask for a more incredible experiment?

I suggested that we try to make the best of it and use this "shortage," so to speak, to our advantage for some research. But no. Ben wanted to play soccer. So, I did what I had to do. I walked into my bathroom, grabbed the pink plastic cup on the sink, turned on the faucet, and filled it to the top.

I walked back into the bedroom and placed it on the nightstand. "Start drinking," I said picking up Ben by one arm and plopping him next to the cup of water.

Ben stared at the plastic cup, which was the same size as he was. "And just how do you suggest I do that?"

It was evident we had a minor problem.

Getting enough water into Ben to dilute the miniature part of the formula was not going to be an easy solution. (So to speak.) I tried to tip the cup, but its mouth was too big and Ben's was too small. He was getting more of a shower than a drink. And he needed more water in him than on him to begin the dilution-and-elimination process.

"Now what, Einstein?" asked a dripping Ben, as he stood in a puddle on the nightstand.

I gave him another tissue. It was clear the cup was not going to do it. We needed some sort of contraption for assistance. Not something overly complicated. Something simple. A straw might be helpful. An eyedropper, even better. Maybe the little cup that comes with the Pepto Bismol?

"Hurry up. I'm freezing," Ben shivered. "I'm only wearing toilet tissue. Wet toilet tissue."

Fortunately, I had the perfect answer to his immediate problem of what to wear. I opened my closet door, knelt down on the floor, and started rummaging in the boxes that were piled in the back.

"Yes! Here it is!" I said, as Ben ducked under a pair of flying jellies.

I crawled out of the closet holding a big dented cardboard gift box, with a smashed corner. I lifted the top and dumped everything on the carpet. "Voilà! Eureka! Get dressed."

"Doll clothes? No way, Gertrude!" Ben leaned over and went eye-to-unblinking-eye with the doll in the bikini. "I am not wearing her clothes,"

"Not hers." I searched under the pile of dresses, bathing suits, and taffeta sequined gowns. "Don't you know anything? She has a boyfriend. See." I pulled him out from under the pile and stood him up next to Ben. "Look. You're in luck. You're almost the same size."

"Yeah, how lucky can I get?"

Ben took a pair of pants and a shirt from my fingers and groaned. I opened my math book and placed it on the floor in front of him. "Your privacy screen," I said, and turned around as Ben put on the doll's pants, complaining the whole time. "I would think you'd be happy not to wear Kleenex."

"I'd be happy if I was back to my normal size. I

have to be home for dinner, Trudie. I think my mother is going to notice that her only son has changed since the last time she saw me, at breakfast. And don't forget about the soccer game. The team is counting on me. Get that brain of yours working and figure something out."

"What's to figure? We know the equation. Water equals dilution equals elimination. We just have to find a way of getting enough water into you to start the dilution process. If we only had an eyedropper or . . ." I looked around the bedroom. "That's it. Get in there with Albert. Take a few gulps from his feeding tube. That should work."

"I AM NOT DRINKING RAT WATER!"

"You want to get back to normal, don't you?"

I placed Ben next to Albert's cage. Albert came closer and gave him a sniff through the bars.

Ben jumped. "Whoa! Hey! He won't bite, will he?"

"Albert is an extremely intelligent rat, Benjamin Bonekowski. He does not bite people. No matter how small they are."

Ben seemed reasonably convinced that Alfred would not think of him as dinner and stepped through the cage door and onto the wood chips. Albert gave Ben a few getting-to-know-you sniffs. While they were getting acquainted, I rinsed the tube and refilled it with new water.

"I really have to drink from this?" Ben said holding on to the bars of the cage and looking at the feeding tube.

"Do you want to play in that soccer game?"

He sucked. He sucked a lot. But—nothing happened.

"Drink some more," I instructed, trying to measure the intake.

Ben took another drink. Another. Then another. He guzzled more drops than Albert sucked down in a week. Still no change. He was drinking, diluting, but . . . Ben was not growing.

Uh-oh.

Chapter 10
A BIG GULP

I put down the ruler. Scribbled some notes. I took off my glasses and sighed.

"The good news is, you are definitely growing. Slowly. But you are growing. You've gone from eight and a half to eleven and three-quarter inches in forty-five minutes. At that rate of growth . . ." I said, hitting the keys on my calculator, "you should be back to your normal size in . . ."

"In a week and a half!" Ben groaned as he sat down on the edge of my desk.

"Stop complaining. So, it's taking a bit longer than we anticipated. We are breaking new ground here. Obviously, the dilution equation is being affected by your size. Maybe we need to tweak the formula a little?"

"No kidding?" cried Ben. "So tweak! Tweak! If I don't grow pretty soon, I'm going to have a rat for a roommate."

"Relax."

"Oh sure. Relax. Notice that I am the only human being in the room who is less than a foot high. And, what do you plan to do when I grow out of these doll clothes?" Ben said, noting that the pants he was wearing were now at his knees and he couldn't button his shirt.

I straightened my glasses and answered calmly. "Not to worry. Under control. You can wear Stuart's clothes."

Ben moaned. "Great. I'm back to wearing diapers."

"Practical for when the elimination part of the experiment starts, remember?"

"This is too embarrassing," he moaned again.

"What we need is another experiment," I suggested, putting on my glasses again.

Ben shook his head. "Uh-uh. No more

experiments. I'm tired of being your lab rat."

"Shhhhh," I said, putting my pinky finger over his mouth. "Albert can hear you."

"Well, pardon me for insulting a rat," Ben said, pushing away my finger. "But—DO SOME-THING."

I, unlike Ben, remained calm, professional, and scientific. I carefully reexamined all of the data, and it was obviously clear that we needed to conduct another experiment. An experiment that would reverse the "mini" in Ben at a very rapid rate.

I tapped my notebook with my pencil. "I think . . . I think . . . Yes, what you need to do is to eat something that will jump-start your metabolism and make you grow quickly. More than quickly. At an extreme rate of growth. Just the way the mini-candy bars affected your system—only opposite in result."

"Like what?"

"Anything really. Just not anything small. Or, medium. It has to be large."

"Large? Yeah. Yeah," Ben squeaked getting excited. "I get it. Giant-size."

"NO!" I shouted with enough breath to knock him over. "Not giant-size."

"Oh. Right. Right. Not giant-size," he said, getting up.

I sighed, put on my glasses, and regained my scientific composure. "For example, a large pizza might do it. Or one of those 'Big Meals.' Something like that."

"So what are we waiting for?" Ben stood up. "Let's eat."

There was only one teeny little problem. (Besides Ben, that is.) How were we going to get "big" food?

And then, Ben—yes, that's right, Ben—had a brilliant idea. Evidently, it's really true what they say. Good things do come in small packages.

"Do you have any money?" he asked.

"I still have the twenty dollars that my grandmother gave me for my birthday," I answered. "Why?"

It was simple.

Order out.

Fast food. Big food. A large pizza. One of those monster hamburgers, a super-size order of fries, and an extra-large drink.

Operation "Big Ben" was, of course, not without its risk. It required precise planning, perfectly timed delivery, and—most important—quick dressing, on Ben's part. But, we were up to the challenge.

We didn't have any choice.

We started to plan. Here's what we knew: my mother, as usual, would be picking up my father at the train station. She would be taking Stuart with her. We would be alone. Result: our window of opportunity to place an order.

As soon as she left with Stuart at 6:15, we would make the call. Delivery usually took twenty minutes.

By my calculations it took fifteen minutes to get to the train station. Five minutes to park. Five to seven more minutes, give or take, for the train to pull in, my father to get off, find my mother, and climb into the car. Then another fifteen minutes to get back home.

That was plenty of time for the food to arrive, for Ben to eat, gulp, and grow. Hopefully, back to normal size.

We looked at the clock. Watched. Waited. Recorded.

6:15 My mother called upstairs that she was leaving to pick up my father.

6:16 I watched the car drive out of the drive-way.

6:17 I placed the order.

6:34 Doorbell rang. Food arrived.

6:35 Ben took off the doll clothing.

6:36 Ben chowed down.

6:39 Ben grew taller than the book screen.

6:39 and one second: I turned around.

6:47 In less than twelve minutes Ben gorged his little body on enough bites of a large pizza, a big hamburger, a super-size fries, and one huge soda to counteract the effect of the seven minia-ture candy bars and return back to normal Ben size.

6:50 Ben put on his clothes.

I didn't look.

Chapter 11

KICKLESS AT MARTIN VAN BUREN

"Kick it, Ben!" Oliver called as he passed cross field. "Kick it."

Ben ran up to the ball, set himself, reared back, and booted. It was a pitiful, sorrowful, puny little kick not even worthy of an effort from Stuart.

"What kind of kick do you call that?" shouted Coach Perkins from the sideline.

"Yeah. Kick it like you did last week, Ben," said Andrew as he ran across the practice field.

We all lined up to practice goal kicks again. Ben walked over and stood next to me.

"One little Wheaties crumb, Trudie. Please. Even a stale Kix. Something."

"BONEKOWSKI!" Coach yelled from the sidelines. "YOU'RE UP."

Ben ran up to the ball and kicked. Another pathetic attempt at the net.

"BONEKOWSKI! What are you doing?" called Mr. Perkins. "Sleepin' out there? This is our last practice before the big game tomorrow. Look alive or you're going to be doing forty laps!"

Ben turned to me. "See what you did? Now your weird science has diluted my natural abilities."

"You didn't drink enough to be diluted," I whispered. "I think maybe all your talents were minimized from the candy intake. Maybe the fast-food worked too fast to return all of you back to where you started and . . ." I stopped talking as Oliver, Andrew, and Matt came running up and huddled around Ben.

"Ben, buddy, come on. Where's that great kick you had last week?" asked Matt. "We need it for tomorrow's game."

"We can't win without you, guy," joined in Andrew.

"Right. Sure. I'm okay," said Ben with a nod. "I'll be fine tomorrow."

"You sure?" asked Ollie. "Were you sick or something over the weekend?"

Ben looked over to me and glared. "No, I wasn't sick over the weekend. But I do feel, what you'd call, a little drained."

"Well, take it easy and get some rest tonight," said Oliver.

Ben looked at me and mumbled, "I'm going to need something a little more than rest."

We lined up for passing and dribbling drills.

Mr. Perkins blew the whistle.

Ben wasn't any better at passing and dribbling than he was at kicking. He passed terribly. He dribbled even worse. Ben just wasn't the usual Ben.

Mr. Perkins gave him twenty laps around the field.

I felt awful. Really awful. So awful, I was ready to do something about it. Watching Ben huff and puff around the track twenty times made me think, it was possible—very possible—that some sort of chemical imbalance could have resulted from all that shrinking and growing. Maybe a bit of cereal couldn't hurt. At least just enough to get Ben's non-formula-enhanced soccer abilities back to where they used to be. I decided to surprise him with the news right after he finished his last lap.

But I was the one who was surprised. Ben didn't want to have anything to do with even a munch of cereal.

"What?" I said, not able to believe what had just come out of his mouth.

"I don't want to use the formula," he repeated.

"Seriously?"

"Totally. Running around out there got me thinking, and I decided you are right." Ben looked at me. "No amazing formulas. Whatever happens, happens."

And that was his final answer.

Chapter 12
BOING!

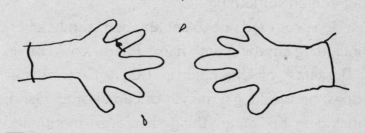

The decision was sealed by a he-spit, she-spit handshake.

"Repeat after me," I instructed. "I, Ben . . ."

"I, Ben," he repeated.

"Do solemnly swear not to eat anything, or do anything in any way, shape, or form that would in any way constitute the definition of *amazing* in regards to the big soccer game. . . ."

"What? What? Slow down, will you? Trudie, I can't remember all of your mumbo jumbo. Can't I just say, I promise not to eat anything and leave it at that?"

We both promised. Nothing edible was going to pass by Ben's lips when I was around from then until after the game was over. And only then, if ever, under very controlled circumstances.

I almost couldn't believe it. Ben and I actually agreed on something.

Ben promised not to eat any hero sandwiches, including anything with ham. There would be no "Breakfast of Champions," Lucky Charms, hot dogs, or sneaking a munch of cereal of any kind, including Kix or anything that even mentioned the word "champion."

He didn't even put up an argument. Ben's rat's-eye view of his Gulliver world and twenty laps around the track had given him a new perspective on fairness. I admit, I got maxed out on mini-Ben and our unpredictable chemistry myself. I also made a solemn oath to also cancel any more experimental "flights."

(For a little while, anyway.)

The only thing was, I hadn't figured on that old "chaos theory." The ripple effect. Some things in the universe just can't be planned or controlled. The moon. The stars. The weather.

And Ben and me.

We just never knew when the weird chemistry between us would . . . well, kick in. We certainly didn't think it was going to happen on the day of the big game.

"Okay, Bulldogs, this is it," Mr. Perkins said as we all huddled around him on the sidelines. "I have confidence in you. Have confidence in yourselves. You can beat this team. If you apply your skills, you're going to play well. When you play well, you give yourself a good chance to come out on top. And that's all any of us can ask of ourselves.

"Just remember what we've practiced. Take the ball around the sides. Don't stay in the middle. And be sharp. Look for your open man. Pass. But, remember, if you get the opportunity, go for the net. That means everybody and anybody. And, kids, try to conserve your energy if you can. It's a hot one today. Okay, let's do it!"

"Feelin' okay today, Ben?" Matt asked as the team took the field.

"As good as I can be," he answered.

"Go, Bone!" yelled Oliver, patting Ben on the back as they ran on to the field together.

"Show 'em how to kick the ball, Ben," shouted Andrew.

"You can do it, Ben," said Zoey.

Ben turned around and looked at me. "I didn't eat a thing. I promise."

"I believe you. I believe you," I said, running alongside of him.

I ran to the middle of the field, and watched Sarah and the center from Mountainview take their positions for the kickoff. The referee placed the ball between them. He blew the whistle and the game began.

Mountainview took possession of the ball and maneuvered toward the sidelines. Ben and I ran up the field and tried to steal or block, but the player from Mountainview darted around us. He was heading for the goal. Our backfield tried to stop him, but he ran past everyone, and before we knew it Mountainview caught our goalie looking the other way, they kicked and scored.

Mountainview 1
Us ☹

It was only three minutes into the game, and we were already behind one to nothing.

We were losing big-time by the end of the first quarter. The score was three zip. It didn't look good. It didn't look like things were going to get any better, either. Mountainview owned the field. Our defense couldn't hold them, and our offense didn't exist. By the end of the third quarter, they had four goals and we still hadn't come close to getting inside the net.

They were running us ragged up and down the field, and the heat didn't help. It must have been one of the hottest days in October on record. Mr. Perkins kept benching and rotating our players to give everyone a rest.

To Ben's credit, he kept his word and didn't have any hidden food backups, or even a few crunches of secret-weapon cereal on the sidelines. If Martin Van Buren was going to win this game, we were going to have someone besides the Amazing Benjamin Bone be the hero.

I had to admit it, though, we could have used him. We needed a hero and soon. Mountainview was crushing us, and it looked like all of us were too exhausted to do anything about it.

Timmy didn't even have to know the score to know that one. He couldn't keep everyone supplied with enough water. It wasn't even the fourth quarter and everyone had already emptied their water bottles. Luckily, Timmy had lugged out a cooler of bottled water onto the sidelines just in case we ran out.

Ben, Oliver, and I were sitting on the bench taking a short breather halfway through the fourth quarter when Timmy tossed us each a bottled water.

"They are too tough," I said, taking a few gulps.

"Come on, we can still beat them," Ben said downing his bottle. "You have to have confidence."

"Ben's right. If we all pull together we can win," said Oliver. "Let's go back out there and do it."

Mr. Perkins motioned for us to go back in as replacements for Andrew, Sarah, and Willa.

"It's brutal out there," puffed Andrew as he chugged off the field. "Make sure you take another gulp of water before you go out there."

Tim tossed Ben another bottle. He unscrewed the cap, took a last gulp, and tossed it back to Timmy. Then Oliver, Ben, and I took our positions as Mountainview tossed the ball in from the sidelines. Somehow, Oliver was able to steal the ball. He maneuvered it down the line and then looked across the field to me. Then he saw Ben. Ben saw him. Ben ran into position.

Well, he didn't exactly *run*. *Bounced* was more like it. Ben was *springing* down the field.

The "Ben plus Trudie" thing was happening again right there on the soccer field! That's right. We didn't plan it. We didn't even want it. We had even taken all of the precautions.

I couldn't figure out what was going on, until I saw Timmy on the sidelines. This time what was happening had nothing to do with what Ben had just eaten. It was what he had been drinking!

It was the H_2O. It was the bottled water Tim

gave us. Ben had been drinking . . . spring water.

Boing!

Boing, oh *boing!* There was no dilution. Only pure spring!

Boing!

Boing!

Chapter 13
HERO SANDWICH

Ben got control of the ball. He took it down-field, covering big yardage with every springing stride. The Mountainview halfback was so stunned by what he was seeing, he just stopped dead in midfield.

Ben cut across into the box. The goal was wide open.

"Kick it!" Mr. Perkins shouted.

"Kick it!" shouted all the parents, teachers, and kids jumping up and down along the side-lines.

"Kick it!" I shouted, running up to Ben.

Ben looked at me and I nodded. He kicked. He scored! We were finally on the scoreboard!

"What's happening?" Ben asked me as we

Kick it!

readied ourselves for the next kickoff. "I didn't eat a thing."

"Spontaneous springing," I told him.

"Spontaneous springing?" he said.

I laughed. "Something in the water."

"What am I supposed to do now?"

I shrugged and grinned. "Go with the flow!"

Mountainview kicked off in midfield. Ben bounded across in front of the left back. He stole the ball and took it straight down the sidelines. He passed to Ollie. Oliver kicked. Nothing but net. We scored again. It was five–two. Then Ben got the ball, dribbled, and leaped down the field and scored again. It was now five–three.

Coach Perkins called in Andrew, who was one of the fastest runners on the team, to replace Grant. Between Andrew's running, Ben's springing, and Oliver's passing, the Mountainview goalie was caught leaning the wrong way, and we scored twice more. It was incredible. We were now tied with only a minute left in the game.

We had a chance to win.

But Mountainview had the ball.

They were moving it down the field. It didn't

look like we were going to be able to stop them. Then Jamie made a great move on their forward and stole the ball. He decoyed his opponent and passed to Oliver.

"Go Oliver! Go!" everyone began cheering.

We were deep in Mountainview territory, in position to score, but then Mountainview took control right back. The clock was winding down. There was less than a minute left in the game.

"Kick it out of there!" we heard their coach shout. "Big high kick!"

Mountainview's star player, who we had already seen kick the ball a mile, set himself for a big one. He reared back and booted the ball hard. The ball started sailing up and over all our players. But Ben was ready. He waited . . . waited . . . waited . . . and then timed his jump perfectly just as the ball came toward him. Ben headed the ball in midair—straight to me!

"Run with it, Trudie," Ben called out. "Run!"

I took control of the ball and ran to the sidelines. I dribbled, then darted, moving the ball downfield, keeping ahead of any Mountainview players. The net was in my view. I was getting close to striking distance. There wasn't much time left. I knew we had to score soon, but I wasn't sure I could kick the ball that far. I looked across the field to find Ben and pass it to him, but I didn't see him anywhere in sight.

"Go for the goal!" I heard Mr. Perkins shout to me. "Kick it!"

"Kick it! Kick it!" shouted everyone else on the team.

Three Mountainview players were in front of me. Two others came out of nowhere. I was sandwiched in between. I had nowhere to go.

Suddenly, Ben sprang in front of me to block. He diverted Mountainview's attention. I had a clear shot.

"Kick it!" Ben yelled. "Kick it, Trudie!"

I reared back and kicked the ball so hard my toes stung.

I watched the ball fly. It was heading for the far left corner of the net. Their goalie stretched out his arms as far as he could waiting for the ball. He waited . . . waited . . . waited as the ball came closer.

Then he jumped.

His fingers tipped the ball, but he couldn't hold on. The ball sailed through to the back of the net.

He missed! He missed!

The ball was in the net!

The referee blew the whistle. The game was over.

We won! Holy Galileo, we won the game! We beat Mountainview. We won the championship!

Everyone was screaming. Shouting. Hugging. Then everybody started jumping all over me. Before I knew it, I was sitting on Oliver's shoulders and being carried across the field.

"You did it, Trudie!" yelled Sarah, giving me a hug on the sidelines.

"Wow, you did. You really did," said Zoey. "I guess you and Ben were really practicing soccer after all."

"Of course we were practicing." Ben interrupted, making his way through the crowd and nudging Zoey. "What did you think we were doing? Hey, you did it, Gertrude," he said, giving me a high five. "You scored the winning goal!"

"With a little help from you," I said with a grin.

"Now, that's what I call great teamwork," said Mr. Perkins, giving us both a slap on the back. "That was some play. You two are a pretty amazing duo, you know that?"

Amazing?

Ben and I looked at each other and laughed.

We were pretty amazing, weren't we?

Ben + Trudie = Amazing

(seriously)

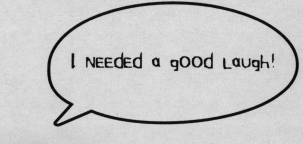